*For my family and
everyone at Victoria House.
J.McQ.*

First published in the United Kingdom in 1997 by
David Bennett Books Limited
United Kingdom

BRITISH LIBRARY CATALOGUING -IN-PUBLICATION DATA
A catalogue record for this book is available from the British Library

ISBN 1 85602 254 4

Production by Imago
Printed in Hong Kong

Cosy Moments
with
Teddy Bear

Jacqueline McQuade

David Bennett Books

Breakfast in bed

As a special treat, Teddy Bear was having breakfast in bed.
He loved toast and jam, but somehow he always
ended up with sticky paws and crumbs on the blanket.

Wearing a favourite jumper

*Teddy went out for a walk in the park.
He felt snug as he kicked through the crunchy
fallen leaves in his brand-new woolly jumper.*

Coming home to hot soup

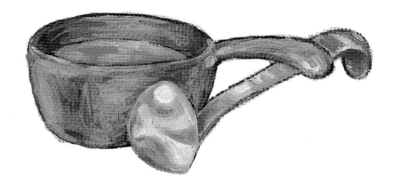

When Teddy got back home, Mummy made some soup
to make him feel all warm inside. Teddy breathed in
the wonderful smell and then he took a sip
of the delicious, hot drink.

Painting
a picture

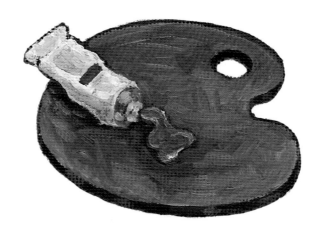

Teddy sat with the cat on his lap
and showed him how to paint a house.
The cat only knew how to do pawprints,
so he was very impressed with Teddy's picture.

Baking fresh biscuits

Mummy carefully took the baking tray from the oven and put it on the table to cool. The sweet smell filled the air and Teddy could hardly wait to try one of the freshly baked biscuits.

Having
a tea party

*When the biscuits were cool enough to eat, Teddy and the cat
had a tea party. Teddy got out the teaset he saved for special occasions:
a pot, a cup and two saucers – one for him and one for the cat.*

Playing
a game

*Draughts was easy when Teddy played against
the cat, but Daddy was much better, so Teddy
had to concentrate very hard on the game.*

Watching
the sunset

Teddy sat with the cat in the amber glow of the setting sun.
"What a beautiful colour!" he thought to himself
as the sun's orange rays filled the sky.

Wrapped up in a soft towel

Teddy had a long soak in the bath. When it was time to get out, he wrapped himself up in a big, warm, fluffy towel. The cat jumped up and snuggled in with him.

Reading
to the cat

After Teddy had got ready for bed, he told the cat a bedtime story.
"This will help you feel as sleepy as me," he said. The cat thought
Teddy read very well, but he wished he could see the pictures too.

A cuddle
with mum

When it was time for bed, Mummy gave Teddy a big hug.
"Sleep well, Teddy," she said. "I love you."

Tucked up in bed

Teddy and the cat were tucked up in bed.
Teddy dreamt of all the things they had done that day
and all the cosy moments they had shared.